DISNEP'S
THE ❧ LITTLE
MERMAID

ADAPTED BY NANCY PARENT

This is the story of Ariel, the Little Mermaid who longed to know love and adventure on land. Read along with me as we embark on an exciting adventure. You will know it is time to turn the page when you hear this sound.... Just follow along and enjoy this wonderful tale about Ariel and friends!

Once upon a time, there was a little mermaid named Ariel who lived in a kingdom far under the sea.

But Ariel was not happy being a mermaid. She longed to be part of the world far above the ocean floor where people lived.

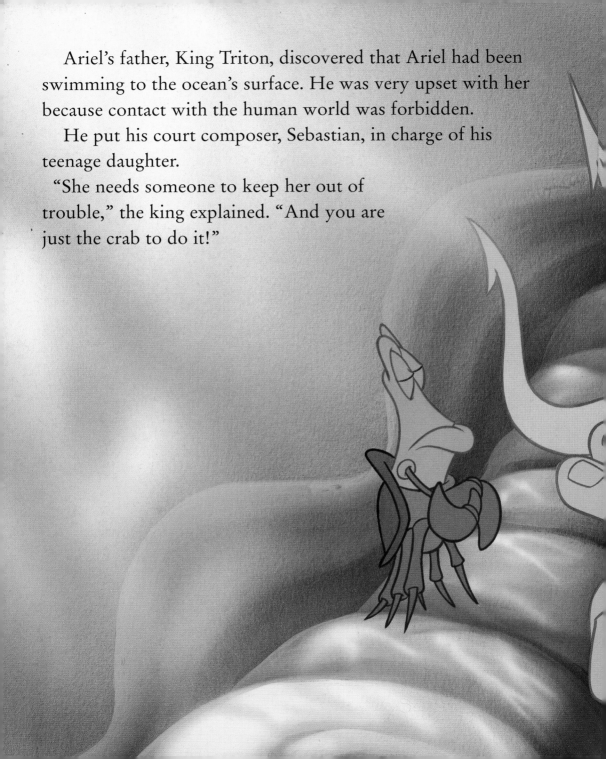

Ariel's father, King Triton, discovered that Ariel had been swimming to the ocean's surface. He was very upset with her because contact with the human world was forbidden.

He put his court composer, Sebastian, in charge of his teenage daughter.

"She needs someone to keep her out of trouble," the king explained. "And you are just the crab to do it!"

But Sebastian could not stop Ariel. One day, she swam up to a ship where she spied a handsome prince named Eric.

Suddenly, a terrible storm came up and Eric fell overboard. Ariel dove underneath the crashing waves and pulled the prince to safety.

Once onshore, Ariel sang to Eric. She thought he was the most wonderful human she had ever seen.

When King Triton found out that Ariel had rescued Eric, he was furious.

"Have you lost your senses?" he asked. "He's a human; you're a mermaid!"

"But, Daddy," Ariel cried. "I love him!"

King Triton refused to listen. But Ariel just had to see her prince again. Later that day, she paid a visit to Ursula, the sea witch.

Ursula promised to turn Ariel into a human in exchange for her voice. She explained that in order for Ariel to remain human, the prince would have to kiss Ariel before the sun set on the third day. "Or you turn back into a mermaid, and you belong to me!" she cackled.

Ariel agreed. Suddenly, her tail changed into legs . . . and she could no longer swim! Sebastian and Ariel's best friend, Flounder, helped her to shore.

When the prince found Ariel, he wasn't sure who she was. He only remembered the beautiful voice of the creature who had rescued him.

"You can't speak?" he asked. "Don't worry. I'll help you."

Eric took Ariel home with him to the palace. On the second day of Ariel's visit, they went on a tour of his kingdom.

But just as Eric was about to kiss her, Ursula's loyal eels, Flotsam and Jetsam, overturned the boat.

Now it was time for Ursula to take matters into her own tentacles. She changed herself into a beautiful girl named Vanessa and wore the shell that held Ariel's voice inside.

As soon as Eric heard the voice, he became hypnotized. He agreed to marry Vanessa that very day aboard the royal wedding ship.

Ariel's friend Scuttle the seagull discovered Ursula's trick. He tried to stop the wedding.

During the struggle, Vanessa's necklace shattered. Eric awoke from his spell, and Ariel got her voice back.

But just then, the sun began to set, and Ariel was turned back into a mermaid. Ursula grabbed her and jumped overboard into the water.

Ursula went right to King Triton. "It's not you I'm after," she explained to Ariel. "I've got much bigger fish to fry."

The sea king offered to trade places with Ariel. Ursula agreed happily.

"At last, this is mine," she cackled, grabbing his crown and magic trident.

Ursula believed she had won.

"Now I am the ruler of all the ocean!" she proclaimed.

But Eric had followed Ariel into the sea. Steering an old ship, Eric aimed the bow right into the wicked sea witch.

Slowly, Ursula's enormous body sank beneath the waves.

Everything returned to the way it was. The ocean became calm once more, and King Triton's power was restored.

The king looked at Ariel's sad face. "She really does love him, doesn't she?" he asked Sebastian.

And, with a wave of his trident, King Triton changed Ariel's tail back into legs.

Soon, aboard the royal wedding ship, Ariel bid her friends and family goodbye. The Little Mermaid had gotten her wish.

She and her prince were about to be married. At last, they would be together forever.